The Best Christmas Ever

The two cats eventually left. Puss didn't even stop to think about it – he raced over and leapt into the bin. He found a kipper head, which was quite tasty, and then half a sausage, but that tasted of soap powder.

Crash!

He nearly jumped out of his fur as the other dustbin crashed to the ground.

It wasn't the two cats back. "It's a fox!"

SYLVIA GREEN

The Best Christmas Ever

Illustrated by Chris Chapman

For my parents

Scholastic Children's Books,
Commonwealth House, 1-19 New Oxford Street,
London WC1A 1NU, UK
a division of Scholastic Ltd
London ~ New York ~ Toronto ~ Sydney ~ Auckland
Mexico City ~ New Delhi ~ Hong Kong

First published in the UK by Scholastic Ltd, 2000
This edition published by Scholastic Ltd, 2003

Text copyright © Sylvia Green, 2000
Illustrations copyright © Chris Chapman, 2000

ISBN 0 439 97762 2

Printed and bound by Nørhaven Paperback A/S, Denmark

2 4 6 8 10 9 7 5 3 1

Chapter 1

I'm Not Staying Here!

"THEY might want to stay in that strange house. But I don't." With two leaps and a bound Puss was across the few paving slabs they called a front garden.

"I'm off home – before Ginger Tom takes over my territory. All that time and effort I put into defending it… How dare they take me away."

The sudden noise of the traffic was deafening as Puss skidded round on to the pavement. He kept his head down and ran. Round the corner and round the next. Over a wall and across a garden.

"And as for shoving me in that basket…" His ears twitched at the indignity of it. He was only usually put in THAT basket to go to someone called Vet. Puss didn't like that either but at least you got to go home again after Vet had stuck needles in you.

"Which way?" He leapt on to a high wooden fence and sniffed the air for familiar smells. "Ah-choo!" The traffic fumes were getting up his nose. "How can you smell anything round here?"

His long black tail swished from side to side as he looked up and down the street.

"Houses. Nothing but houses. Where are the fields? Where are the trees?"

He cringed as yet another lorry thundered by. "Ye-owl!" Puss was used to a few cars coming through his village but this was dreadful – they never stopped. "Why on earth did Jenni want to come and live HERE?"

He spotted a tabby cat sitting on the bonnet of a red car that was parked in a front garden. "I'll ask him where the fields are."

Puss jumped down and padded over to the cat, his tail gently curved in a friendly manner. "Excuse me." He thought he'd better be polite – after all he was a stranger here.

The tabby cat immediately stood up and arched his back. His fur bristled to the end of his tail. "Ssss-stay back!

Keep your distance!" he spat. "Don't even think about trying to take over my territory."

Puss jumped back. "How rude." No cat in his village would have DARED to speak to him like that. They knew their place – they respected him. Well, Ginger Tom did try it on sometimes – but he soon sorted him out.

"Call that a territory?" Puss gave the hissing, spitting cat his Special Stare. "What would I want with a tiny patch of gravel with a car parked on it?" he growled. "And only one measly bush? You should see my territory – it's ENORMOUS. It's got LOADS of bushes. And trees to climb and lots of grass…"

The tabby cat wasn't interested. He crouched down and let out a low, warning yowl.

Puss gave an irritated flick of his tail. "It's no use asking HIM anything. He's obviously got no idea about the finer things in life."

With his head held high, he stalked off. Puss – the fearless cat – had never needed anybody's help before. "And I don't need it now," he said.

Round the corner there was a row of different buildings. Puss stared up at the big windows full of gold and glitter.

"Shops." He'd only ever seen the village shops from the car on the way to see Vet. And he'd never taken much notice – he was too busy sulking at having been shoved in THAT basket again. But he knew about the shops – that was where Jenni's mum got his cat food.

He broke into a run. "The fields will be just up here. And then I'll be home."

He gradually slowed down as he got past the shops. There were no fields. Just more houses.

These were not the village shops.

He kept walking, ears pricked for familiar sounds. "How can I hear the cows mooing or the field mice squeaking with all this traffic?"

He glanced down to check his white front feet. His boots, Jenni called them. She often called him Puss in Boots because he was all black with four white feet. His boots were definitely looking grubby but he couldn't stop to wash them now.

"They actually expected me to STAY at that house," he grumbled. "Telling me I had to get used to it and then I could go out in the back garden. Call that a back garden? That tiny square of grass I saw from the window? Huh! I'm going back to my OWN garden – my OWN territory."

He stopped and looked all around him. Nothing was familiar – he couldn't see anything he recognized.

Then, through the traffic, he caught a glimpse of something ginger on the other side of the road. It was a cat.

"It's Ginger Tom!" cried Puss. He actually felt pleased to see him. "If he's here then home must be just around the corner. I bet he's on his way to try and take over my territory right now. I'll show him."

He tried to get across the road to him. But the traffic just didn't stop. There was only one thing for it. He put his head down and made a dash for it.

There was a terrific squeal of brakes. Horns tooted. A man fell off his bike and shouted at him – Puss had never been called THAT before!

Somehow, he made it to the other pavement. He was breathing hard and his heart was beating fast. The cat was sitting on a fence watching him.

It wasn't Ginger Tom.

Chapter 2

Where Are You, Puss?

"Puss! Puss!" Jenni's throat was getting sore from calling. "Oh, where can he have got to?"

"I should have checked those boxes before I opened the door," said her mother. "I know how Puss likes boxes. But the way he shot out – so fast – it was almost as though he'd planned it."

"He probably had," said Jenni. "He

hates being shut in. If only he'd waited till he was used to his new home. Now the poor little thing's got himself lost."

Jenny's mother shivered in the cold December air. "We've been searching for two hours now. I think we should go back and have a hot drink."

"No. You go back if you want to," said Jenni. "I've got to keep looking for him."

"But you'll get lost too, on your own," said her mother. "We haven't even been in East Deeming for two whole days yet."

"I'll be okay," said Jenni. "All I have to do is look for that really tall office block and I know our house is just round the corner."

As she set off again she looked at all the unfriendly people who just walked by without speaking to anyone. In the small village where they'd lived before everyone knew each other and stopped to say, "Good morning" or "How are you today?"

She knew Dad felt bad about them having to leave their village – and all their friends. But he'd had to move with his job. It wasn't his fault.

"Puss. Puss," she called, for probably the five-hundredth time. She passed two girls about the same age as her walking along chatting together.

The children round here have already got their own friends, she thought. I'm dreading starting my new school after Christmas. I wish I wasn't so shy.

In the next road she spotted a tabby cat, sitting on the bonnet of a red car. It stood up for her to stroke it.

"Hello," said Jenni. "You're a nice friendly cat. I wonder if you've seen Puss. If only you could talk."

She walked on looking into all the tiny
front gardens. She peered under all the
parked cars. Everywhere felt so strange –
so closed in. She missed the big open
fields – and all the animals.

"I shouldn't think there are any animals living round here – apart from the odd cat or dog," she said to herself. "I so loved helping Mr Roberts get his cows in for milking. And collecting the eggs with Anna – and feeding the chickens and geese." She gave a big sigh. "There's nothing to do round here."

Just round the corner was a row of shops. The windows were bright with Christmas decorations. But they did nothing to cheer her up.

Jenni shivered. "Perhaps I should go back for a hot drink. And maybe – just maybe – I'll find Puss has come home on his own."

But Puss wasn't at home.

Jenni's mother had gone back to unpacking the huge boxes of their belongings. She was anxious to get the house straight before she started her new job after Christmas.

Jenni begged her to phone the people that had bought their house in the country. "You do hear of cats and dogs turning up at their old homes," she said.

"I know you do, dear," said her mother. "But we've moved over three hundred kilometres. He might be a clever cat, but even Puss couldn't find his way back there."

Jenni quickly swallowed a cup of hot chocolate and opened the front door to go out again. A movement caught her eye. It was a pigeon pecking at something in the road. Jenni watched in amazement as it expertly side-stepped the cars.

"Wow! All this traffic obviously doesn't bother you," Jenni said to it.

"But there can't be anything for you to eat round here."

She fetched it some bread and the pigeon raced towards it. He hungrily gobbled it all up and even took a piece from her hand.

Jenni smiled. "At least something is friendly round here," she said.

"We'll all make new friends eventually," said her mother. "And try not to worry too much about Puss. I bet he's trying to find his way back here right now."

Chapter 3

An Even Worse Place
Than Jenni's New House

"The sooner I get away from this dreadful place the better." Puss padded through the big shopping precinct and the mass of human legs. He knew these shops DEFINITELY weren't the ones in the village. These were HUGE. And one of them even had stairs that moved up and down all on their own!

"Ye-owl!" Puss put his ears back and scampered past. "That's not natural."

Puss was hungry. His long black tail swished from side to side. "Not one mouse to catch round here. This is no place for a fearless hunter like me."

There were people everywhere. He padded along trying to dodge the hurrying boots and shoes. "Miaow. Watch where you're putting your big feet.

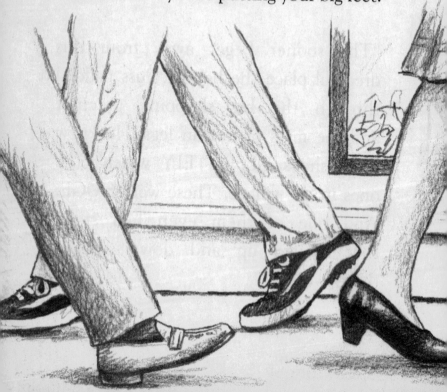

Mind my beautiful tail." But at least there weren't any cars or lorries here.

A movement in a low shop window caught his eye. He stood up on his back feet to get a better look. "Wow! Puppies. And kittens. And birds."

A little brown puppy with a black nose looked up at him. Several others were asleep on top of each other. "What are you doing in there?" asked Puss.

"And why are you shut up in cages? Is this some sort of animal prison?"

The puppy obviously couldn't hear him through the glass. Puss watched a guinea pig in the next cage scurry round in the sawdust to hide behind its brother.

The door opened and a lady came out with a boy who was carefully carrying a small box. "Thanks for buying me this mouse, Mum," he said.

Puss pricked up his ears. She'd bought him a mouse! You had to pay for them round here! No wonder he couldn't find any.

The boy spotted him. "Look, Mum," he said. "D'you think that cat has escaped from the pet shop?"

Puss didn't wait to hear any more. "I'm off. I'm not going to be taken in THERE.

They're not shutting me up in a cage — and I've got no money to pay for mice."

There were fewer people about now and it was starting to get dark. Puss turned into an alley behind the brightly-lit shops. His eyes quickly adjusted to the darkness and he spotted some cardboard boxes. "I'll curl up in one for a while, keep warm and have a rest."

But there was someone there. Inside a large box, on its side, Puss saw a young man lying covered up with an old blanket.

"What's he doing? It looks as though he's in bed. Surely he can't live HERE? This is an even worse place than Jenni's new house."

He watched the young man take something out of a bag and begin to eat it. Puss's sensitive nose twitched.

He could smell cheese. He liked cheese.

The young man looked up and spotted him. "What's up, mate? You not got anywhere to go either?"

He looked nice – and the cheese smelt good. Puss ventured closer.

"Are you hungry?" The young man broke off a piece and held it out. "It's only a stale old cheese sandwich. It's a bit hard but if you're as hungry as me you'll eat anything."

Puss cautiously took the piece in his mouth. He'd never had a sandwich before. He watched the young man carefully as he chewed on it. It tasted okay.

They finished the sandwich between them and the young man patted the blanket. "Come on. We can keep each other warm."

Puss snuggled up to him in the cardboard box. In this cold unfriendly place at least there was someone kind – and warm.

When he woke up the next morning, just for a minute, Puss thought he was back home curled up with Jenni. Then the young man moved him to get up and he felt the cold. He blinked at the bleak alley-way.

The young man folded his blanket and picked up his bag. He stroked Puss. "I'm off now. Goodbye, mate. Thanks for the company." He walked to the end of the alley and stopped to look in some dustbins. Then he was gone.

Two scruffy-looking cats sauntered up to the dustbins. Puss darted back into the box and peered out at them. One had long matted black fur and a torn ear. He jumped up and knocked the lid off one of the bins. It clattered to the ground and both cats leapt in.

The scruffy tortoiseshell cat, which had no tail, jumped out with something in its mouth. It was bacon – Puss could smell it. Then the black one followed with some fish.

Puss watched in amazement as they tore at their meal, looking round them all the time. The young man had looked in the dustbins too before he left. "Is this the way you eat in towns? And you have to pay for the mice. This place gets worse all the time."

Puss edged out a little and sniffed the air again. The bacon smelt good. His mouth watered. "But I'd NEVER lower myself to eat out of a dustbin. It's too degrading."

The two cats suddenly spotted him. They hissed at him. "Ssss-stay back. This is ours."

This was obviously their territory. Puss retreated into his box – the fearless cat wasn't in the mood for a fight this morning. "Of course, I could beat the two of them easily – if I wanted to."

The two cats eventually left. Puss didn't even stop to think about it – he raced over and leapt into the bin. He found a kipper head, which was quite tasty, and then half a sausage, but that tasted of soap powder.

Crash!

He nearly jumped out of his fur as the other dustbin crashed to the ground.

Puss cautiously peered over the top of his bin.

It wasn't the two cats back. "It's a fox!"

He prepared to run. Then he realized the fox wasn't taking any notice of him. It was tucking into some vegetable peelings that had spilled out of the bin.

"Yuck!" said Puss. "Foxes never do have good taste." He decided to make his escape and jump down while it was busy eating.

But the fox glanced up at Puss, and then it moved over so he could join him. Puss was amazed. The foxes in the country hadn't been friendly at all.

They ate side by side as Puss discovered some tasty bits of cheese rind and a half-eaten hamburger. The hamburger took a lot of chewing – Puss wasn't surprised it was only half eaten.

He felt quite good after his meal. "Now I'm going to find my territory." Beyond the dustbins he could see the shopping precinct where he had been the night before – but at the other end of the alley, in the distance…

"A tree," cried Puss. "I'm almost home."

He bounded off towards it, leaving the fox to finish his breakfast on his own.

Chapter 4

I Didn't Know
You Got Wildlife in Towns

Jenni had missed Puss's soft damp nose being thrust into her face as usual to wake her up in the morning. Not that she'd slept – thinking about him out in the cold, lost and hungry.

She shivered in the early morning cold. The shops weren't open yet in the shopping precinct but several people were scurrying off to work. A movement in an alley caught her eye.

"A fox," she breathed. She stood and watched it eating from an overturned dustbin. "It's beautiful."

The fox had spotted her and was watching her carefully but it kept on eating. Jenni was amazed to be so close to a wild creature. The foxes in the country hardly ever came near the houses and were very shy of humans.

Jenni took a poster out of her bag. She'd made it yesterday evening on the computer and run off twenty-five copies. Even though people weren't friendly round here, she hoped they'd read them and contact her if they spotted Puss.

She'd headed the poster PUSS IN BOOTS in big black letters to give an immediate description of the little black cat with four white feet.

A woman stopped to look at it. "Are you in it too?" she asked.

She took Jenni by surprise. "Pardon?"

"The pantomime – *Puss in Boots*. I haven't seen you at rehearsals."

"Er – no. I'm not," said Jenni.

"Didn't think I'd seen you," said the woman. "Just helping out with the posters, are you?"

She didn't wait for a reply but hurried off.

"I don't believe it," cried Jenni. "Someone's putting on the pantomime *Puss in Boots*. People will just think my posters are an advert for the pantomime." She looked at the poster. Why did they have to be doing *Puss in Boots*? Why couldn't it have been *Cinderella* or *Aladdin*?

Then she had an idea and folded over the top bit with PUSS IN BOOTS on. "It's not so eye-catching but it still makes sense," she decided.

"Lost. Black cat with four white feet," read a voice over her shoulder. She turned to see a woman peering at the poster. "That your cat, love?"

"Yes," said Jenni.

"I'll keep a look out for him," said the woman. "And have you thought of asking your neighbours to check their sheds? He could be shut in somewhere." Then she was gone. But two people had actually spoken to her!

"I'll ask Dad to come with me this evening to knock on all the neighbours' doors," Jenni decided.

She went back and adjusted the posters she had already put up. Then she stuck the rest of them up around the town. A pet shop in the shopping precinct put the last one in their window for her.

On the way home for lunch she spotted a neighbour just coming out of her house carrying a pile of Christmas presents.

Jenni didn't even stop to think about being shy. "Excuse me," she said. "I've lost my black and white cat, and I was wondering if you could look in your garden and in your shed – if you've got one."

"Of course I will," said the woman. "My own cat went missing last year but she turned up at the animal shelter in Sycamore Street. Have you tried there?"

"No," said Jenni. "I didn't know about it. Thank you."

The animal shelter was housed in a large, old, dingy building but inside it looked surprisingly bright and cheerful.

Jenni stood silently with her fingers crossed on both hands as the receptionist checked their records.

She finally looked up. "No. I'm sorry, your cat hasn't been brought in here."

She smiled at Jenni's sad face. "I'll make a note of his description – and your name and telephone number. Then if he is brought in I'll give you a ring."

"Thank you," said Jenni. A box on the counter suddenly started rustling.

To Jenni's amazement the receptionist reached in and lifted out a small hedgehog. "Ah, the warmth's woken you up, has it?"

"Shouldn't he be hibernating?" Jenni asked.

"He was," said the receptionist. "Under a bonfire. A boy spotted him and rescued him just before his father lit it. But this little chap's actually too small to go right through the winter. They need to be quite big to be able to survive a whole winter's hibernation. So we'll keep him warm and feed him up."

Jenni stroked the tiny head. "You don't just take cats and dogs then?"

"No. We've got a wildlife wing. We've got rabbits, badgers, all sorts of birds including owls and several foxes."

"I saw a fox this morning," said Jenni. "I didn't know you got wildlife in towns."

"Oh yes, you just have to look a bit harder for it," said the receptionist.

Jenni had an idea. "I was wondering – after I've found my cat – do you need any helpers here? I love helping with animals."

"I'm afraid you're too young yet," said the receptionist. "Hey, don't look so disappointed – in a couple of years we'll be glad of your help." She handed Jenni a piece of paper. "This is a list of things we always need here – things like newspapers and old towels for the animals' cages and runs. Perhaps you could get your mother to save some for us."

"Oh yes," said Jenni. "And I'll bring them in."

"And don't give up hope for your cat," she told Jenni. "It's early days yet."

"I won't," said Jenni. "I'm going to keep searching for him until I find him – no matter how long it takes."

Chapter 5

Puss Makes a Friend

Puss left the railway embankment – and the tree that he'd seen from the alley-way. "That's definitely not my territory."

He put his ears back and scampered off, as yet another train thundered past behind him. "What a racket!" He was amazed the noise hadn't bothered the badger he'd just met. It actually lived in its sett, right there, on the banking.

A few streets further on, Puss spotted more trees in the distance. He instantly cheered up. "That's it. That's bound to be my territory."

The dingy street opened out to a grassy area – but it wasn't what Puss was expecting – it was wasteland. There were a couple of trees, and plenty of grass, but there was also brick rubble lying around and the remains of a building.

"Rabbits!" Puss watched them scampering around and eating the grass. He liked rabbits. Back at home there was a white one called Arabella living next door. He loved to sleep on top of her hutch.

Suddenly all the rabbits disappeared down their holes.

A loud barking from behind told Puss why. He jumped round to see a large black dog racing towards him.

"Ye-owl!" He wasn't keen on dogs at the best of times. And this one was ENORMOUS. Puss – the fearless cat – pulled himself up on fully stretched legs and arched his back to make himself look bigger. He hissed and spat as he gave the dog his Special Stare. Then he lashed out with his paw as an extra warning to leave him alone.

The dog hesitated. But then it lunged forward with its HUGE red mouth wide open. There was only one thing to do in this situation. The not-quite-so-fearless-cat now turned tail and fled into the ruined building. But the dog followed.

Puss ran out again. The dog followed.

Puss raced round the bricks. The dog followed.

He couldn't outrun this dog. He spotted a small gap in a wall. His sharp senses immediately told him he could get in but the dog couldn't. He dived through it but a sharp piece of brick tore at his fur. "Ouch!"

There was a thud as the dog crashed into the wall. "Stupid dog," said Puss. "Fancy trying to get through that hole. A cat wouldn't make that mistake."

"Butch! What are you doing now?" A man's voice came from outside.

Through the hole in the wall Puss gleefully watched the dog stagger towards its master. It was obviously dizzy from the bump on its head.

The man spotted Puss and gave a laugh. "Well, Butch, I see you've met your match this time. Perhaps this will teach you not to chase cats." He made a quick inspection of the dog to make sure he wasn't injured, then he put his lead on and tied him up to a dead tree stump.

Butch made an instant recovery and started barking.

The man bent down to Puss. "Come on out, Puss," he coaxed. "Let's see if you're all right."

"He called me Puss. I don't know him, but he seems to know me – perhaps he'll take me back to my territory." Puss ventured out of the hole.

He even allowed the man to pick him up. "That's good," said the man as he looked at him. "Apart from a bit of missing fur, you're not injured." He brushed the brick dust off him. "There you are, that's better."

Puss stared down at the dog from the safety of the man's arms. It was barking furiously now – obviously jealous.

He rubbed his head under the man's chin and grinned to himself as his actions made the dog bark even more.

"You're a lovely puss, aren't you?" said the man, stroking him. "But where have you come from? I've never seen you round here. I know all the cats." He looked down as Butch gave a frustrated whine. "So does Butch."

Puss was disappointed. He didn't know him after all.

"Are you lost?" the man asked him. "I can't take you home with me, because of Butch. But I could take you to the animal shelter. At least you'd be warm and fed, shut up in there."

Puss had heard enough. "He's not shutting me up anywhere." He leapt out of the man's arms and raced across the grass. "If I'm shut up somewhere I'll never find Jenni," he panted. What was he thinking about, find Jenni? "I'm looking for my old territory," he corrected himself. "I'm not going back to that DREADFUL house, even if Jenni is there."

Puss found himself on the canal bank. He spotted a bridge and raced across it. Butch and the man – thank goodness – didn't follow him.

He was in a big yard. A crane was loading planks of wood on to a barge on the canal. Puss scampered round the back of some piles of wood.

A movement caught his eye. His senses were alert immediately. It was a mouse! A FREE mouse. He hadn't caught a mouse for AGES.

Puss automatically sprang into action, crouching low and silently, stealthily moving forward. He'd lost none of his skill.

A quick, excited wiggle of his bottom and he pounced!

The mouse didn't stand a chance against the fearless hunter.

A white cat suddenly appeared round a pile of wood and Puss was quick to safeguard his catch. He arched his back, his fur standing on end, and hissed at the intruder. "Ssss-stay away. Keep back. This is my catch."

The cat was holding a piece of bread in her mouth and she dropped it in front of

him. "I don't want your mouse. I've caught three already this morning."

Puss relaxed a bit. "Three?"

The mouse took advantage as Puss loosened his grip. It made a break for freedom and scampered off into a woodpile. The first mouse he'd caught in ages – and this silly town cat had made him lose it.

"There are hundreds more round here," said the white cat. "I'll catch one for you if you like."

"No." The fearless hunter certainly didn't need another cat to catch a mouse for him. "I can easily catch one myself – that one was a bit small anyway. Did you say there were … hundreds … round here?"

The cat nodded. "And the men often give me titbits." She pushed the piece of bread towards him with her paw. "Jim just gave me this – he always shares his lunch with me. Would you like it?"

Puss's nose twitched. It was a piece of cheese sandwich. He chewed on it hungrily. He was getting to quite like cheese sandwiches.

The white cat purred and rubbed herself against him. "Why don't you stay here with me? We could have some fun together."

Chapter 6

It's Puss's Fur!

First thing the next morning Jenni went out to buy a street map of East Deeming. She wanted to put some order into her search, make sure she didn't miss anywhere.

The pigeon was waiting for her when she got back. And it had brought two of its friends with it.

Her mother laughed. "It didn't take you long to find something to feed."

Most of the neighbours had been friendly when Jenni and her father had knocked on their doors last night. They'd agreed to search their gardens and sheds for Puss. Only one old man was grumpy. He told them he hated cats as they dug up his garden.

Mrs Armstrong from number eight told her that her own cat had been hit by a car last month. But it had managed to get home and she had found it hidden in a pile of leaves in the garden. "They often hide away if they're injured," she told Jenni.

Jenni couldn't bear to think of Puss being hurt. But he wasn't used to these dangerous roads. She had to find him soon!

Jenni studied the map for places Puss might have gone to. "There's somewhere I should try." It was an alley-way behind the houses in the next road.

"Puss. Puss." Jenni walked along the alley-way, stopping nervously to examine every pile of dead leaves. She looked into the gardens on either side.

A lady putting food on a bird table looked up as she heard Jenni call Puss. "You must be the little girl who's lost her cat – I saw your poster. He's all black with four white feet, isn't he?"

Jenni nodded. "I call him Puss in Boots."

"What a coincidence," the lady chuckled. "That's the pantomime they're putting on over in Manningford this year. Have you seen the advertisements for it? Have you seen the advertisements for it?"

"Yes," said Jenni. "Mum said that

perhaps my Puss has gone to seek my fortune – like the one in the pantomime did for his master. But she was just trying to cheer me up."

"I'm sure he'll turn up soon." The lady asked Jenni her name and introduced herself as Mrs Baxter.

Jenni liked her. "Do you get many birds round here? I've only seen pigeons so far and a couple of starlings."

"Oh yes," said Mrs Baxter. "A lot come into the towns in winter. It's warmer you see – all the buildings give a bit of shelter."

"And people like you feed them," said Jenni.

"Yes, I put out wild bird food and scraps like cheese and bread. That's for birds like sparrows, starlings, blackbirds and robins," said Mrs Baxter. "Peanuts and bacon rind attract blue tits, great tits and greenfinches. Oh, and squirrels."

"You get squirrels in the garden?"

"A couple of them. Cheeky little things. But they're hungry too so I don't mind them having some of the peanuts."

"I like squirrels," said Jenny. "And birds. I like all animals really."

A little girl with long blonde hair popped her head over the fence. "I like animals too. D'you want to see my rabbit?"

Jenni went into her garden. She was called Alice and was a couple of years younger than Jenni. Jenni admired Alice's fluffy black and white rabbit. She told her how she'd just moved from the country with her family and that Puss had gone missing.

"I saw something in a pile of leaves just now," said Alice. "Over there. It was moving so I was afraid to look."

Jenni's heart raced as she bent over the pile. It was moving, slowly, almost as if the heap was breathing. Her hands shook as she parted the leaves.

"Ouch!" She pulled her hands away quickly. Something had pricked her. "It's not Puss," she told Alice. "But I think I know what it is." She carefully scraped more leaves away to reveal a large hedgehog curled tightly in a ball.

"Oh, lovely." Alice clapped her hands. "Is he all right?"

"Yes he's fine. He's hibernating," Jenni explained, as she covered him up again. "He's nice and big so he'll be all right to sleep right through the winter."

Alice looked impressed. "I suppose you know that because you used to live in the country."

Jenni smiled. "No, actually I learnt that yesterday. Here, in the town."

"Will you come and see me again?" Alice asked.

Jenni smiled. "Of course I will."

After lunch Jenni decided to search by the canal. It wasn't far according to the map and it was the only bit of open space nearby. Puss was used to open spaces.

Her mother came with her. "It might be nice by the canal," she said.

"I doubt it," said Jenni. "This is a canal

– in a town. Not a lovely river like we had in the country. It's probably filthy and full of rubbish."

She was in for a surprise though. The water was clean and clear and there were ducks, geese and swans swimming on it.

Jenni smiled. "I'll bring some bread the next time we come."

They watched a long colourful narrowboat going past and a barge being loaded up outside a wood yard on the opposite bank. The towpath on their side was edged with grass and bushes. A small group of people were cutting back some overgrown trees.

They went to ask them if they'd seen Puss.

"No, sorry," said a young man. "We've only just got here. We'll keep a look out though."

There were a girl and a boy who looked a little older than Jenni and they smiled at her. She smiled shyly back. "What are you doing?"

"We're members of CWAG," said the boy.

"That stands for Canal and Wasteland Action Group," added the girl. "Lots more of us come at the weekends. The group has cleared the canal of rubbish and made it usable again."

"But it's taken a long time," said a lady.

"Several years. And we're always looking for more volunteers. There's loads more to do."

Jenni's mum looked interested. "What a wonderful idea. We'd love to help, wouldn't we Jenni?"

The girl smiled at Jenni. "Yes, why don't you join us?"

Jenni smiled back. "I'd love to. But I've got to find my cat first."

The young man gave them a leaflet about the group. Then he suggested they try searching on the adjoining wasteland.

Jenni went there straight away. She ran amongst the bricks and rubble. "Puss. Puss. Are you here?"

She was amazed to see three wild rabbits scampering round the remains of a building. She ran after them, but they had disappeared.

Then she caught sight of something in a hole in the wall.

"It's black fur," she cried, pouncing on it. "Here, caught on this brick. It's Puss's fur."

"Don't get your hopes up too much," warned her mother. "It could be from anything."

"It is Puss's fur," cried Jenni. "I know it is. He's here. Or at least he was here. He can't be far away."

Chapter 7

Spaghetti Bolognese

Puss had been walking for two days. He didn't know where he was. He could have been walking round in circles for all he knew. And he was starving!

"I should have stayed with that friendly white cat," he grumbled to himself. "There was plenty of food – and it was quite nice there." He put his ears back as he set off again. "But it wasn't home.

And I'll never find my territory if I don't keep looking. Fearless cats don't give up that easily."

He'd found a few titbits on a rubbish dump, which he'd shared with a family of foxes and about two hundred screaming seagulls. But that had been yesterday morning.

Then he smelt it. A really delicious meaty smell. His mouth began to water. The smell was coming from behind a sort of shop. "Perhaps there's a nice old lady there like the one who used to give me titbits back at home."

The smell got stronger as he made his way down the side driveway to the back. There was a delivery van parked there and a lot of shouting coming from the shop. Puss cautiously peered round to see what was happening.

A man in a tall white hat was doing the shouting. "I've-a been waiting for this spaghetti for over an hour." He was very red in the face. "I'm-a famous chef, you know. The customers love-a my delicious, out-of-this-world, home-made Spaghetti Bolognese."

"I'm sorry," said the other man. "I couldn't find your restaurant."

The chef followed him out to the van. "All-a the meat is cooked and waiting. But Spaghetti Bolognese I cannot make-a without spaghetti."

Puss put his head on one side. He could see the cooked meat on a worktop just inside the door. He sniffed the air and breathed in the delicious smell. The kitchen was empty. "Surely he won't miss a little bit of it."

The chef was still shouting at the man as they looked in the back of the van. "Now's my chance." As quick as a flash Puss was inside the kitchen and on to the worktop. He gulped down two mouthfuls of the warm Bolognese sauce. The chef was right – it was delicious.

A scream made him drop his next mouthful. The chef's face, in the doorway, had turned almost purple now. He was spluttering and spitting as though he couldn't get his words out.

Puss leapt down and cowered in a corner as the chef threw a ladle at him. "You-a vile animal. You-a hateful, flea-ridden, filthy bit of vermin. How-a can I give that to people now?"

Puss shrank back as a saucepan lid came towards him. He didn't see why he couldn't give the meat to people. It had tasted all right to him – and he'd only eaten a little bit.

The chef advanced towards him with a HUGE saucepan in his hand. Puss had seen enough. He shot through the chef's legs and skidded out of the door. The saucepan clattered down behind him as he raced round the side of the restaurant.

"I'll-a get you for this," screamed the chef after him. "I'll-a search for you till I find you. I'll-a make you sorry."

Puss didn't stop running for a long time. Then he sat down to get his breath back and to have a good wash. "What a fuss," he said, as he licked his right foot and rubbed it over his right ear. "I only had two mouthfuls. There was plenty left." He carefully licked all along the black fur on his back. "How dare he call me vermin. And especially FLEA-RIDDEN and FILTHY. I've got a beautiful coat – Jenni says so."

He felt a twinge of sadness as he thought of leaving Jenni behind. She'd probably miss him. And she'd miss the mice he used to bring in for her. The look on her face when she saw them made all his efforts worthwhile. She had such fun chasing them all over the house.

He quickly shook himself. He had to get on. He finished cleaning each of his white boots and set off again.

He walked and walked. He crossed another canal – or was it the same canal but a different bridge? This place was so confusing. One time he thought he recognized a very tall building but then he wasn't sure.

"I can't be losing my touch. Does hunger make you confused?"

Puss spent the night in an alley-way behind some houses. He curled up in a pile of leaves under a bush. At least it was away from the traffic.

A small terrier dog woke him up in the morning. She yapped at him through her gate. "Come and play. Come and play," she called. "I've got a ball. I've got a ball."

She looked friendly enough – even though she was a dog – but Puss couldn't stop to play. He had to get on with finding his territory. "I bet Ginger Tom is having a good laugh about taking it over."

He jumped up on to the wall of the next garden to see if he could spot anything familiar – or even something to eat. "What's that?" It was a rabbit in a hutch. But Puss saw immediately it wasn't Arabella. This one was black and white and a little girl with long blonde hair was talking to it.

He ran along the wall to the next garden and lots of birds flew off. Jenni didn't allow him to chase birds.

"Why do I keep thinking about Jenni?"

Puss sniffed the air. "Bacon. And cheese." He looked over to a bird table. Jenni often put bits of food out for the birds. He'd never bothered about it before – never lowered himself to eat the birds' scraps. "But I've never been this hungry – and there might even be a cheese sandwich."

He jumped down and started to make his way across the grass. Then the back door opened and a lady came out. She gave a gasp as she spotted him. "Well, my-oh-my. Fancy seeing you here."

Puss hesitated. He was sure he didn't know her.

"Come on then," she coaxed. "Come here, boy."

Puss took a step towards her. She looked nice and there was a smell of cooking coming from the house.

"Good boy," she said. "Come on. There's someone looking for you. Been searching everywhere, they have."

"Ye-owl!" Puss stopped immediately. The mad chef had people out looking for him. He turned tail and ran. Out of the garden. Down the alley-way. Down the next street, over a fence and out on to the road.

There was a deafening squeal of brakes as a car skidded towards him.

Chapter 8

Poor Little Cat

Jenni studied the map. Puss hadn't been on the wasteland or along the canal – or anywhere else in the surrounding area. She'd been back again and again.

There was a knock at the front door and she heard her father go to answer it. It was Sunday and he'd promised to spend the morning helping her search.

"Perhaps it's someone with news of Puss." They were getting to know quite a few of the neighbours now. They often asked after Puss and even stopped for a chat. Mum said it sometimes took an animal to get people talking.

"Jenni."

Jenni looked up to see Mrs Baxter, who had been feeding the birds yesterday. She was out of breath and looked excited. "I've seen him – Puss in Boots. All black with four white feet. In my garden – ten minutes ago."

Jenni jumped up. "Oh, thank goodness. Where is he? Did you catch him?"

"I'm sorry, but he ran away from me."

Jenni jumped up and grabbed her coat. "Was he all right?"

"He looked fine," said Mrs Baxter. "Come on, I'll help you find him."

Jenni's father joined them and they raced round to Mrs Baxter's garden.

They searched up and down the alley and in all the gardens. Alice and her mother came out to help and so did a lady with a small terrier dog. They looked round all the surrounding streets – but there was no sign of him.

Jenni didn't want to go back for dinner but her father insisted. She was upset and frustrated. "He can't have got far. Oh, why did he run off again?"

After dinner Mum and Dad were going to the canal to join the members of CWAG. "Your father's already phoned to say we'll be there," said Mum. "So we've got to go. And at least you know Puss is okay now. He can't be far away. Why don't you come with us? You've been searching non-stop for five days."

"No," said Jenni. "I've got to keep looking for him."

As soon as they'd left Jenni put on her yellow and black trainers. She smiled as she looked at the tiger's face on the toe. Puss had been so funny the first time he'd seen them, pouncing on them then jumping back and pouncing again. She was going to thoroughly search the whole area again – he was somewhere nearby. He couldn't have gone far – she was bound to find him this afternoon.

Then the phone rang. "I've just seen a black and white cat," said the voice on the other end. "It was knocked down by a car in Market Street, I'm afraid. I think it might be dead."

"Oh no!" Jenni uttered a garbled "Thank you" and put the phone down. She grabbed her coat and flew out of the door. She knew the area so well now she knew exactly where Market Street was.

It was only two roads away but it seemed miles as she raced round there. She felt sick with worry and guilt. "I shouldn't have gone home for dinner. I should have stayed out looking – I bet he was knocked down while I was actually eating."

She turned the corner into Market Street. "Oh, please, please let him be all right."

Her eyes immediately focused on a small black and white body lying in the gutter. "Oh no!" She raced towards it. He was so still – he looked... She couldn't bring herself to even think the word.

She dropped down on her hands and knees. She was shaking badly as her eyes rapidly took in the black and white fur.

It wasn't Puss.

"Oh, thank goodness." Jenni was still shaking, but an immense feeling of relief flooded over her. Puss wasn't dead. He was still missing – but he wasn't dead.

"Poor little cat," she whispered to the tiny bundle in the gutter.

She heard footsteps running towards her and stood up to see a boy of around her age.

"Saskia!" he cried. He turned to Jenni, his eyes wide with pain. "That's my cat."

"Oh, I'm so sorry." Jenni felt terrible as she looked at him. She'd been so relieved it wasn't Puss – but of course it had to be someone's cat.

The boy was obviously trying hard not to cry. "I don't know what to do. Mum and Dad are out."

Jenni felt so sorry for him. She reached out and put her arms round him to give him a hug. "What's your name?"

"Mark."

Over Mark's shoulder she blinked back the tears herself as she looked down at the poor little cat.

It twitched!

It twitched again.

"She's not dead!" she cried.

Mark appeared to be frozen to the spot so Jenni took charge. "Where's the nearest vet?" she asked, tearing off her coat.

"In the next road," said Mark. "What are you doing?"

"Help me," said Jenni, laying her coat out on the pavement. Together they carefully lifted Saskia on to the coat and Jenni wrapped her up in it to keep her warm.

Mark had pulled himself together and led the way as they ran round to the vet's. All the way Jenni was willing the little bundle in her arms to hang on – to stay alive.

The vet was called Miss Williams and she immediately connected Saskia to a drip. "It's to counteract the shock," she explained, as she covered the little cat up to keep her warm. "The first thing is to get her over the shock and then we can find out what injuries she has and treat them."

They had to leave her there. Miss Williams said it was just a matter of waiting to see if she came round.

Jenni walked back with Mark to his house. He wanted to wait in, in case the vet phoned. "Thanks, Jenni," he said. "Thanks a lot for your help."

Jenni gave him her phone number. "Please let me know how Saskia gets on. I've got to go now as my own cat's missing and I've got to keep searching for him."

"Oh, I'm sorry," said Mark. "Have you tried looking over the council rubbish dump? Or the wasteland?"

"I've tried everywhere," said Jenni. "But I'm trying it all again and again. I've got this strange feeling that I keep on just missing him."

Chapter 9

Missing Jenni

Puss was really fed up. He'd walked miles and miles and there was no sign of his old territory. But to his surprise he found he wasn't so bothered about that now. He was missing Jenni. Oh, how he was missing Jenni. And he didn't know how to find her again.

He stood and watched the traffic. He was learning to be more careful –

a car had only just missed him the other day when he ran into the road. And yesterday he had heard some people talking about a cat that had actually been hit by a car. In somewhere called Market Street. He didn't know if it was dead or not but apparently a boy and a girl had taken it to see Vet.

"Wait a minute." He had a sudden thought. "If Vet is nearby maybe I can find him. Although I was always taken there in the car... But then I was brought here in the car too. It seemed a bit longer getting here – but it must be the same place."

He pictured the large man in his white coat as he set off along the pavement again. "He should be easy enough to recognize. And he's bound to remember me – he said he'd never forget me after my last visit. Well, who could blame me for wrecking his surgery? The embarrassment of it!"

He gave an indignant twitch of his tail as he remembered something called a thermometer. He hadn't known where to look when Vet had stuck it into his bottom!

"One or two broken bottles and a few scratches were nothing to the embarrassment I suffered. It was all right for Vet telling me it was the usual way to take an animal's temperature. It wasn't him standing there with a thermometer stuck in his bottom." Puss paused. Did he actually want to see Vet again?

"Yes," he decided, setting off. "When Vet sees me he'll phone Jenni and she'll come and get me."

Puss stopped for a rest. He'd walked along countless streets. Past houses and shops, over bridges, under bridges, in and out of alley-ways. But there was no sign of Vet.

"It's a wonder I haven't worn my feet out, walking on all this hard ground," he said. "I'm sure my legs are getting shorter."

He was so tired and so hungry. He was beginning to feel weak from lack of food – and he'd had a fight with a big black tom-cat. And he'd lost! The fearless cat had never lost a fight in his life before.

"Of course he was EXCEPTIONALLY big," said Puss. "And he had obviously had an ENORMOUS dinner – so I didn't stand a chance." He sat down to lick his sore leg where the big bully had bitten him.

"I can't think why he was so aggressive – that tiny square of grass he called HIS garden was hardly worth defending."

He stood up as a group of youngsters came towards him. Perhaps Jenni was with them. They stopped right next to him and he quickly looked up at all the faces.

She wasn't there.

"Have you seen Puss?" one of them asked.

Puss's heart jumped. They must be friends of Jenni's. They were looking for him. He immediately ran forward, his tail held erect. "Miaow. I'm here."

They didn't hear him. The trouble is, my deep, throaty, masculine cry is a bit weak these days, he thought.

"I think he's going to meet us there," said a boy.

"Where?" Puss panicked as the group moved off chattering excitedly. "Where's THERE? Where am I supposed to meet them? And will Jenni be THERE too?"

He'd have to follow them. He limped after them, through a huge gateway and into a sort of field with grass and trees. But cars were driving through it and there were strange creatures in the distance with huge antlers on their heads.

"Funny looking cows," said Puss.

It seemed a long way and Puss was exhausted. Only the thought of finding Jenni again kept him going.

They eventually stopped outside a hall.

"There he is," said a girl. "There's Puss."

"At last!" Puss looked up expectantly. But the girl was pointing at a boy. A SILLY boy with big boots on and whiskers drawn on his face. "Come on," said the boy. "The pantomime's due to start in an hour."

Puss didn't know what they were talking about. But he did know it wasn't him they were looking for. And Jenni wasn't there either.

He was tired, weak and very, very hungry. There was a cardboard box next to the hall door and he dejectedly crawled inside. Somehow, the fearless cat – the fearless hunter – just didn't feel fearless any more.

It started to snow. Puss remembered snow – he usually liked to play in it. But not this time.

He curled up in the box to keep warm and watched the snowflakes falling thickly outside. "I'd have been better off staying at THAT house," he murmured. "At least I would have been warm and fed. And I'd have been with Jenni…"

Chapter 10

Jenni's Treat

"It's starting to snow," Jenni's mother called to her. "We're going to have a white Christmas."

Jenni looked out of the window. She remembered Puss in the snow last year. He was so funny, jumping up and down in it and trying to bite it. She thought about him all the time.

The brightly decorated Christmas tree

made her think of him trying to climb it when he was a kitten. And of him jumping up to catch the silver and gold baubles. He'd actually knocked the tree right over one year.

Wrapping her presents for Mum and Dad reminded her how he loved chasing the ribbon as she tried to tie it. Jenni didn't want any presents this year – all she wanted was Puss.

"Christmas Eve," she sighed. "And still no sign of him. This is my worst Christmas ever." Jenni put her trainers on again – they'd be good for gripping on the snow. She tried hard to keep her spirits up but it was getting harder and harder as the days went by.

"You're not going out again in all that snow, are you?" asked her mother. "You've been out all morning and you've only been in for ten minutes to eat your lunch."

"I've got to keep searching," said Jenni. She opened the front door and threw some bread to about fourteen pigeons waiting on the paving slabs. A couple of sparrows had joined them today. "And I'll be going out again tomorrow – Christmas Day. I won't give up."

"I'm just a bit worried about you. You're not getting any rest," said her mother. "I'll help again later, when I've finished icing the Christmas cake." The phone rang and she went to answer it.

Jenni waited. It might be about Puss. So many people were concerned about him now. Every time Jenni went out someone stopped her to ask if there was any news. People were so much friendlier round here than she'd first thought.

And the area didn't seem so bad now she was getting used to it. She'd seen several more foxes, and a couple of squirrels searching for their winter store of nuts. Even a badger when Dad took her to the railway embankment one evening.

Dad was making her a bird table and they were going to have a pond.

Mr Samuels from number twenty-four had told them that garden ponds in towns provided essential breeding sites for frogs and toads. There were fewer sites in the countryside now as ponds and ditches were filled in. And hedgehogs were finding more food available in people's gardens – more and more wildlife was adapting to living in towns.

The canal area was nice and the wasteland would be nice too when the members of CWAG had converted it into a nature park. But without Puss she couldn't appreciate anything.

"Jenni. Wait a minute." Her mother called from the phone.

Jenni's heart leapt. "Is it about Puss?" Perhaps it was the animal shelter to say he was there, safe and sound. But she'd already been there this morning to drop off some newspapers and he hadn't been there then.

"No. It's Mark, for you. I've just been chatting to his mum."

Jenni rushed to the phone. "It'll be about Saskia."

"She's going to be okay," cried Mark. "Saskia's broken a back leg and she's got bruising to her lower back – but she's going to recover. We've just brought her home."

"Oh, I'm so pleased she's all right," said Jenni.

"Well, it's mainly thanks to you. Miss Williams said if you hadn't acted so quickly Saskia would probably have died of shock," Mark told her. "Mum wants to give you a treat to say thank you. Can you come round?"

"Oh, I don't know…" said Jenni. She looked up at her mother.

"Mark's mum has already asked me if it's okay," said her mother. "You go. You deserve a treat. And you need a break. Dad will be home early today and then we'll both go out and look for Puss for you."

"All right," Jenni agreed. "Thank you," she said to Mark down the phone. "I would like to come and see Saskia."

Saskia was a lovely cat. Her markings were quite different to Jenni's Puss with his boots. Saskia was black with white on her face and throat and two white legs and feet. And one pink leg – that was the broken one in plaster.

Mark was the same age as Jenni and was very nice. "I'll help you search for your cat after Christmas," he told her.

His mother was nice too. She was

taking them out, but she wouldn't tell Jenni where – it was a surprise. Jenni would much rather have carried on looking for Puss but Mark and his mother were being so kind to her. She'd have to try and enjoy herself for their sake. And she was pleased to have made a friend.

They were going by car, as it was quite a long way. The windscreen wipers swished away the snowflakes that were falling steadily now.

"We're going through the park," said Mark. "Have you been there? It's just into Manningford – it's very nice."

"No I haven't been out of East Deeming," said Jenni. "I've been too busy searching for my cat."

She looked out of the window as they drove through the park. It did look nice.

There was a lake and she saw a herd of fallow deer in the distance. At the moment it looked rather like a scene on a Christmas card with all the snow on the bare branches of the trees.

They drove out of the park on the other side and pulled up outside a hall.

"We're here," cried Mark. "I'm really looking forward to this."

As they walked towards the gate, Jenni looked up at the big colourful banner above the door. It read:

THREE O'CLOCK TODAY
CHRISTMAS PANTOMIME
PUSS IN BOOTS

"Oh no." Jenni stopped and stared at it in horror. This was to be her treat. To watch *Puss in Boots*! Tears welled up in her eyes. She couldn't sit and watch it – not with her own Puss in Boots missing.

"What's the matter?" asked Mark.

"My cat – the one that's missing. I – I didn't get a chance to tell you before – but I call him Puss in Boots."

"Oh no," said Mark. "I'm so sorry – I didn't know."

His mother put her arm round Jenni. "Would you like me to take you home again, dear?"

Jenni nodded. Then she looked at her watch. "But it's three o'clock – the pantomime's just starting. If you take me back now, you and Mark will miss it too."

Chapter 11

The Best Christmas Ever

Puss shifted in his cardboard box. Something had woken him, disturbed him. People had been going past for ages. But this was different – it was something familiar.

"The voice. It's Jenni's voice!" He uncurled himself and peered out of his box. "Miaow. Jenni, I'm here."

Where was she? She couldn't have

heard him. If only his voice wasn't so weak now.

He crawled stiffly out of the box. A group of people were just coming up the path but she wasn't with them.

Then his sharp hearing picked out Jenni's voice again. "I can't make you miss the pantomime – it wouldn't be fair. Mark just said he was looking forward to it," she was saying. "I will come in. I – I expect I'll be all right."

Puss's sensitive ears immediately located the direction – Jenni was just behind these people.

He shot off down the slippery path. As he skidded towards the group, he caught a glimpse of Jenni through their legs. "She's there – down by the gate!" He frantically tried to dodge round the hurrying feet but he slipped on the trodden snow. Then a HUGE boot kicked him.

"Ye-owl!" Puss was knocked off his paws. He rolled over and over down a bank until he came to a halt up against a bush.

He scrambled to his feet again and shook himself. "I've got to get to Jenni."

But the huge boots had followed him. "Are you all right?" A man picked him up and began brushing the snow off him. "I hope I didn't hurt you."

Puss couldn't wait around to be comforted. He had to get to Jenni. So he did the only thing he could – he bit the man's hand to make him let go.

Once free, he clawed his way back up the bank, gripping on the grass beneath the snow. The rest of the people had gone now and he raced down the path. He skidded to a halt at the gate.

Jenni had disappeared. "Where is she?"

Puss spun round and saw her. She was at the top of the path now – almost up to his box.

He raced back up the slippery path. "Miaow. Jenni! Miaow."

Puss reached the top just as Jenni disappeared into the hall.

Suddenly there was a big burst of music and people were clapping. Puss hesitated and put his ears back. "What a noise." But he had to go in there. "I've got to get to Jenni."

"Hey!" shouted a lady as Puss squeezed through her legs.

It was a huge place – so noisy and so many people. Where was Je—?

"Ye-owl!" Puss was suddenly swung into the air as the lady grabbed him by the scruff of his neck.

Then he was outside again.

"Sorry, we don't allow cats in here," said the lady, and laughed. "At least, not real ones."

Puss yowled and wriggled and squirmed in her grip. The man with huge boots appeared in the doorway. "I think that cat's wild," he said, as he went into the hall.

Puss was dropped down into the snow. Too true he was wild. And furious. He immediately scrabbled round again to get back in. But the lady was too quick for him. She closed the door in his face.

He scratched and scratched at the door until his claws hurt. But no one let him in. They probably couldn't hear him anyway with all that music and clapping and shouting. "What on earth's going on in there?"

He crawled back into his box. "I'll just

have to wait for Jenni to come out again. She's got to come out sometime."

Puss settled down to clean off his fur with one eye firmly fixed on the door. He was tired, hungry – and completely exhausted. His side hurt from the kick and he ached all over. But he couldn't go to sleep. "I mustn't miss Jenni coming out."

Puss fought hard to stay awake but his eyelids kept drooping. "Why doesn't Jenni come out? What's she doing in there?" His head nodded forward.

Puss was jolted awake as laughing, chattering people streamed out of the hall. But all he could see was a flurry of boots and shoes kicking up the freshly fallen snow. He panicked. "I'll never find Jenni in all this. Why have so many people come out at the same time?"

Had he missed her already? He joined in amongst the mass of legs moving down the path towards the gate. He couldn't see past them and he certainly couldn't see up to any faces.

Then, ahead of him, through a small gap, he spotted something familiar. Yellow and black trainers with a tiger's face on them. "Jenni's shoes!" But she was way ahead of him – she must be almost at the gate.

"Miaow. Jenni! Miaow." She couldn't hear him. "I've got to get to her.

If she goes without me, I might never find her again."

Puss desperately tried to push his way through the mass of legs.

"What's going on?" said a lady.

"It's a wild cat," said Huge Boots. "Watch your ankles – he bites."

Puss got past him as he stood aside. Then he managed to push past several more people. They were all moving so slowly – but at least that meant he wasn't so likely to be kicked. If only he could get through…

He squeezed between a boy's legs. Then, at last, he was at the gate.

But Jenni had gone. "Where is she?" Puss frantically looked around him.

"Oh no. She's in that car. She's leaving."

Somehow, Puss gathered together every last bit of strength he had left.

He raced forward and jumped up on to the bonnet just as the car started to move off. His claws screeched on the slippery paintwork as he fought to steady himself.

The lady in the driving seat screamed. The car shuddered to a halt.

Then the doors were flung open and Jenni was there. "Puss!" she shrieked. She was laughing and crying at the same time as she picked him up. "Oh where have you been? And look at you, you're so thin."

Puss snuggled into her. His side hurt where Jenni was squeezing him but he didn't care. He was with Jenni again – his Jenni.

A boy was jumping up and down on the pavement. And the lady was saying something about getting them home.

Then they all got into the car. Puss purred and purred as he settled down on Jenni's lap. She was as soft as he remembered and she smelt so nice. She was stroking him and kissing him on his head. "Oh, I've missed you so much," she said. "I do love you, Puss."

Puss usually got embarrassed with all that sort of thing – but today he didn't care.

"I can't believe I've found you at last," said Jenni, tickling him behind his ears – just the way he liked it. "Although it was really you who found me. But whatever are you doing here? It's such a long way from home. However did you get here?"

Puss pushed his head under her chin and thought to himself that it was something to do with a mad chef chasing him. And a silly boy with big boots on and whiskers drawn on his face.

"You know what?" Jenni started to laugh. "The Puss in the pantomime went off and found riches and good fortune for his master. And in a different sort of way that's just what you did for me. Through searching for you I've met friends and neighbours – and I've realized it's not so bad round here after all. And there's lots to do."

"And don't forget about Saskia," said Mark. "If you hadn't been searching for Puss you wouldn't have found my cat and helped me with her."

"No," Jenni agreed. "This is Mark, Puss. He's my friend. You'll like his cat – she's called Saskia."

Mark grinned at Puss. "You're a fearless little cat, aren't you? Jumping up on a moving car like that."

Puss snuggled into Jenni's lap. The boy was obviously intelligent – he'd realized straight away what a fearless cat he was. The woman looked okay too. And anyway, he'd just made a decision. From now on anywhere Jenni wanted to be was okay with him.

"And there's a nice rabbit that lives just round the corner," Jenni told him. "You like rabbits, don't you? This one

126

belongs to Alice – you'll like her too. Then there's a friendly lady who feeds the birds…"

Puss closed his eyes as Jenni talked softly to him – and purred even louder. He was actually looking forward to going back to his new home. To being in the warm and to lots of good food. And at least he had his own territory there.

All right, so the back garden's a bit small, he thought. But it'll take me less time to defend it – give me more time to spend sleeping.

And as soon as I'm fit again, he decided, I'm going to find that black tom-cat. Sort him out, show him who's boss round here.

Jenni gave him a big cuddle. "You're all I wanted for Christmas. This is the best Christmas ever." She gave him another kiss. "Happy Christmas, Puss in Boots."